Taking

Young People and Risk-Taking Behaviour

Arthur Brown
Lecturer in Youth Ministry and Applied Theology,
Arab Baptist Theological Seminary, Beirut
and BMS World Mission Worker

GROVE BOOKS LIMITED
RIDLEY HALL RD CAMBRIDGE CB3 9HU

Contents

First Impression June 2009
ISSN 1748-3492
ISBN 978 1 85174 724 5

1 Introduction

As I watched Tony speed past on his motorbike, front wheel pointing skywards, I wondered how he had learnt his trademark skill of 'popping wheelies.' While envying his skill (being a biker myself), part of me feared for his safety and the trouble he could encounter with the police. Earlier that week I had taken a group of young people kayaking at the local water sports centre. Having nearly drowned (twice) whilst paddling down white rivers in the past, I was very aware of the potential risks involved. And yet we all had a great time, and really bonded as a group. Walking home involved crossing a busy East London road, which was maybe the most risky thing we had done all day. Living in Shadwell with its gangs, prostitution, cheap drugs, crime and often poor education was risky. And yet this was the adventure God had called my family and me to.

The fact that we now live in Beirut may tell you something about our attitude towards risk. As we watched the Royal Navy ships approach Lebanon to evacuate British citizens during the 2006 war between Israel and Hezbollah, following Jesus took on a new meaning. Our calling to Lebanon had been clear. Having returned to the country 24 hours before the bombing started, our call to stay seemed even clearer. Living through the 34-day war, experiencing the devastating destruction of communities where friends lived, watching and hearing bombs land in built up areas of the city, four kilometres from our home, was horrific. However, when we had left the UK in 2005 one thing that saddened us was some of our Christian friends asking if it was safe—as if safety was a prerequisite for following God's lead. Yes things can, and do go wrong. We could have been harmed—physically, emotionally or spiritually—by remaining within a war zone. However, would that have meant that we were not meant to have been there, or that we were not abiding by God's will? I think not!

Some Christians see safety as a prerequisite for following God's lead

I have come to the conclusion that for his followers, the fullness of life Jesus refers to in John 10.10 involves the highs and the lows that come from being prepared to take risks for and with Jesus. Following Jesus involves a spirituality of risk-taking—a spirituality of fearlessness, that holds onto possessions, lifestyle, security and even safety lightly. However, this type of spirituality appears alien to a world caught up with self-preservation, fear, financial security and individual achievement. Interestingly, the financial markets are based on risk. The more we are prepared to risk our financial savings, the more dividends they might pay. Maybe the global financial crisis can teach us something of the dangers of seeking security in risky financial institutions and practices. Maybe we can also see the paradoxical nature of our faith. Jesus may ask us to give up our safety whilst offering us belonging in him that is eternally secure.

Jesus may ask us to give up our safety whilst offering us eternal security

Our experiences might seem extreme to some, but we feel privileged with the life God has given us and that we live it to the full—that is not to say perfectly, but with successes and failures. Faithfully following Jesus in any setting—rural, urban, in the UK or overseas, at work and in the local community—carries risks. Risk is a part of life, and an even greater part of the Christian life.

Young people are often associated with risky behaviour. I have often been asked why young people do 'such stupid things,' why they seem preoccupied with hurting themselves and others. However, many reports about youthful risk taking behaviour are misleading. This booklet is not an examination or explanation of young people's risky behaviour, but rather seeks to explore why some young people are willing to take significant risks so we can better understand their needs and develop appropriate responses.

Understanding Risk Taking Behaviour

2

Gullone and Moore define risk taking as '...the participation in behaviour which involves potential negative consequences (or loss) balanced in some way by perceived positive consequences (or gain).'[1] Currently Britain demonstrates a marked disparity in how risk taking is perceived. On one hand we see many young people participating in risky (sometimes anti-social) behaviour. Media frequently demonize young people for participation in gang violence, drug and alcohol abuse, sexual promiscuity, car and motorbike theft etc. without considering those involved. However, a report for Play England suggests that many youngsters are denied adventurous play.[2] 51% of children polled were forbidden to climb trees without adult supervision for safety reasons.[3] Society has mixed ideas about risk-taking, so young people receive inconsistent messages.

Examples of 'Risky Behaviour'

Below is a non-exhaustive list of activities or experiences many young people participate in. Some are riskier than others, some are socially more acceptable than others. However, all contain degrees of risk, whether physical, emotional or social.

- Participation in certain sports (climbing, BMX, skateboarding, boxing, rugby...)
- Walking home alone, late at night
- Having unprotected sex with multiple partners
- Smoking cigarettes
- Crossing the road
- Being a gang member
- Injecting heroin
- Carrying a weapon (knife, bat, gun...)
- Hanging around on the street at night
- Climbing trees/jumping across streams
- Disruptive behaviour within a peer group context
- Using ecstasy at weekends
- Driving a car or motorbike recklessly
- Fighting
- Entering into a romantic relationship

- Playing in an adventure playground
- Being a member of a family in which domestic violence and/or other forms of abuse take place
- Smoking cannabis
- Spending time with certain friends
- Drinking excessive amounts of alcohol on a regular basis
- Being in a class with a school bully
- Sniffing glue
- Self-harming behaviours (eating disorders, cutting, attempted suicide
- Stealing
- Playing 'chicken' on a road/train track
- Vandalism
- Uncontrolled access to the internet
- Following Jesus?

What Makes Activities 'Risky'?

Most human activities involve elements of risk; however, some are considered riskier than others due to:

- The likelihood of harm occurring (high, low, moderate risk of harm);
- The severity of that harm (potential for minor injuries such as scratches or bruises, potential for severe and permanent injury or death); and
- The potential benefits to be experienced through participating in a specific activity or activities.

The harm might or might not be physical. If you were asked to evaluate the risk associated with the above activities, which would you consider more or less risky?

The Glamis Adventure Playground in Shadwell had become derelict and unsafe. Members of Cable Street Community Church and other local residents (with significant support from the local Play Association), formed a management committee to explore the possibility of redeveloping the playground for the local children and young people. After much work, funding was secured to appoint a team of workers (full and part time) to develop the playground into a place where children from the multi-cultural community could learn to play together, breaking down racial and social tensions. Whilst the church did not manage the project it was instrumental in bringing the playground back to life, a vision it has for the local community in general. Glamis Adventure Playground recently won the award for London Adventure Playground of the Year.

Perception is Everything

Focusing on potential physical harm arising from participation in such activities is easy. However, the potential for emotional and psychological harm should not be forgotten. This type of harm is possibly more prevalent in many young people's minds.

Young people today inhabit different worlds from those many of us knew. There is more awareness of potential risks within society. Adult perspectives, which fail to consider what is going on in the minds of young risk takers, dominate research and reporting about risky behaviour. If we do not understand what motivates young people to risk harming themselves, we cannot understand them or their needs. Therefore criticism of their actions as destructive will cause us to miss opportunities to become involved with them. Young people do not need more criticism; they need people willing to get alongside them, to listen and respond. This is where youth workers, mentors, pastors and professional or non-professional carers have crucial roles. Rather than just responding to behaviour (the visible tip of the iceberg), we should look below the surface.

We must acknowledge risk taking as part of adolescence. If infants do not risk falling they never learn to walk. Children who never risk drowning never learn to swim—a potentially life-saving skill. Whilst watching my four-year-old daughter climbing the tree in our garden sometimes causes my heart to miss a beat, I know it is a natural part of her development. The Play England report suggests limiting opportunities for young people to experience risk-bearing activities may hamper development. Much research and experience suggests that 'wrapping a child up in cotton wool' reduces opportunities for developing social skills including independence, self-awareness, confidence, critical thinking and decision-making, and the ability to cope with challenging situations in adulthood. Risk avoidance can obstruct young people's development.

Risk avoidance can obstruct young people's development

We must be well informed when considering potential consequences of risky behaviour for young people, who often look to youth workers and others for guidance. When it comes to risk taking behaviour, a simple 'don't do it because it is dangerous' is unacceptable to curious minds receiving different messages from influential peers. We also need honesty and realism. For example, the reality is that smoking cannabis occasionally is unlikely to cause lasting damage, whereas habitual cigarette smoking may incur lasting harm. The accepted social and legal activity is riskier. Without encouraging cannabis use, we should recognize that it is safer than other activities young people participate in such as sniffing glue.

A crucial question is, 'To what extent do you think a young person's conscious or unconscious choice to participate in risk taking behaviour is rational?' Can, and do, young people weigh the pros and cons of participating in a fight before the event and base their involvement on such evaluations? Or is young people's risk-taking behaviour purely irrational? Your answer will affect your understanding of young people and affect your responses.

We generally look at adolescent risky behaviour from an adult-centred perspective. Adults frequently concentrate on likely negative results of risk behaviour/s (unwanted pregnancy, potential for physical harm, involvement in the criminal justice system). They often focus on what is socially acceptable to their peer group as well as the law. But young people often consider potential positive outcomes from participation in 'risky' behaviours before considering harmful consequences. Therefore we must examine how participation in certain activities may be presented positively. Instead of focusing solely on the worst thing that could happen, we may need to consider the best thing that could happen in any given situation.

By taking common risk behaviours and exploring how they may appear to non-participating adults and participating young people, we might gain insight into why young people choose to do such things. Perhaps we will need to reconsider the rationale behind youthful risk taking.

> *One Eighty* is a mobile skate project, run by Bath Youth for Christ. Its mission is to 'Relevantly and contextually proclaim the gospel of Jesus Christ through words, actions and example to young people who are a part of the skate culture and community of Bath,' aiming to provide regular indoor skate facilities, information, advice and support for young people and an opportunity for them to explore themselves and the Christian faith. *One Eighty* are involved in local detached work and have developed a 6-week course called *Thrive* which can be run in schools, 'Helping young people learn life skills through skateboarding, rollerblading and BMX bike riding.' (www.180.resolvesolutions.co.uk)

Risk activity	Negative adult perception	Positive perception from a young person
BMX riding	Potential for injury Anti-social (fear of groups of young people) Potential for damage to the environment	Image of being tough Excitement Satisfaction in learning new tricks Sense of community/belonging Fitness Prestige Self-expression/feeling of freedom
Gang membership	Potential for harm caused by violence Negative peer influence Likelihood of involvement in criminal activity Reduced likelihood of educational achievement Potential loss of family reputation	Image of being tough Power, influence and control Significant degree of belonging to a peer group Opportunities for fun/buzz activities Expression of rebellion against 'oppressive social structures' that have potentially failed an individual (school or other authorities)
Alcohol and drug use	Potential damage to health Loss of control/reliability/ability to make sensible choices Anti-social behaviour Potential involvement in criminal activity	To have fun/get a buzz To dampen pain (emotional/ physical...) To fit in with the crowd To appear adult
Promiscuous unprotected sexual activity	Danger of sexually transmitted disease Emotional damage Potential for unwanted teenage pregnancy—reduction of life opportunities Potential loss of family reputation	Desire to feel loved and cared for Need to be included within sexually active peer group Need to prove masculinity or sexuality to self and/or others Inquisitive to know what sex is really like Emulate media role models Desire to have a child, and become a mother/father
Following Jesus	Challenge to parental authority/ influence Time and energy put into 'church' activities rather than home or study Potential financial contributions towards activities, camps, mission trips The need for personal sacrifice rather than individual development	Personal relationship with God Purpose and meaning Self-worth as a result of relationship with God Close knit community Values and beliefs worth fighting for Radical political agenda
Self-harming activities	Physical and psychological damage Risk of death	Release internal tension Need to fit in within a peer group[4] Image conscious (need to be a certain weight/look a certain way) Gaining a feeling of personal control Gaining attention

Driving cars/riding motorbikes recklessly	Risk of physical harm/death Anti-social behaviour Potential involvement in the criminal justice system Potential loss of family reputation	Fun/buzz factor Symbolic identity (speed freak/ wheelie man/skilful rider...) Expression of rebellion
Disruptive behaviour within a group setting (eg youth club/ group; school classroom etc)	Limited opportunity for education, development and growth Disruptive influence on others Source of frustration, hopelessness and anger to group facilitator	Opportunity for self-expression/ fun Symbolic identity (clown/joker; powerful leader) Opportunity for rebellion within safe contexts Expression of boredom

Potential Positive Consequences?

Participation in risk activities indicates expectations of positive consequences. Recognizing this increases our willingness and ability to understand young people when considering their participation in such practices. This will enhance our ability to offer support in reducing potential significant lasting harm or death.

Some Further Considerations

Morality and social ethics have significance in decisions to participate in some risky behaviours. Such decisions are determined by how the young person views an activity and the consequences of involvement. Research indicates that adolescents often view substance abuse as a matter of personal choice, whereas theft and violence are moral issues. However, many young people today do not recognize the wider social consequences of their actions and are unwilling to forego personal freedom to participate in activities they enjoy in order to benefit others.

Many young people discount factual knowledge about the potential harm of participating in an activity, particularly when perceived benefits seem significant and immediate. Many risky activities, like drinking, sex and violence, are interrelated. Trying to reduce participation in one may do little to reduce potential harm in others. Rather than focusing on one particular activity or behaviour we should develop lasting and consistent relationships with young people involved in risk-taking behaviour, thereby gaining insights into their worldview.

Young people willing to break laws or social conventions in one area are prone to do so in another. Thus 15-year-olds who are willing to purchase alcohol might be more likely to smoke cannabis with friends. Whilst this may be negative, there is also a positive side. Young people may be willing to break social conventions in order to demonstrate justice or challenge inequality. Maybe young risk-takers better understand the subversive nature and activities of Jesus and are, like him, more prepared to flout unjust social conventions in order to remain true to their beliefs and values.

Perhaps young people can show us a spirituality that is categorized by a willingness to take risks, as they hold on to things lightly, including at times their own safety. Young people often talk about the desire to be free, and maybe it is risk-takers who are able to be free, as a result of their spirituality and perception of what is valuable. Fear is not a dominating, debilitating or limiting feature of their existence, which allows them the freedom to live life 'to the max' (John 10.10). The willingness to sacrifice oneself, like the shepherd may need to, in order to be identified as a member of something greater than the individual, is a constant theme throughout Christian faith communities.

3 Why Do Young People Take Risks?

Young people take risks expecting benefits. What motivates this behaviour? While reading the following case-studies, consider young people you know and their participation in risky activities.

Aaron is 19 and lives in East London. He has had few temporary jobs since being excluded from school when 14. He smokes and drinks heavily, and steals and rides motor-bikes with friends. Some of his associates habitually carry knives. Because of racial and territorial conflicts in the area the group stays within its neighbourhood. There is no local youth provision because of recent cut-backs.

Sarah is the 15-year-old daughter of a prosperous suburban Birmingham family. She lives with both parents, and occasionally attends the youth group of the church where her mother worships. An older sister went to university two years ago. Sarah's parents have jobs that involve long working hours, including some weekends. She spends much time alone at home or in the homes of friends. Some weekends they go to parties with older boys, some of whom legally own and drive cars. At parties some girls drink half a bottle of vodka each. Sarah has had protected sexual intercourse with two older boys, once whilst under the influence of alcohol. Recently two of Sarah's friends began self-harming by cutting themselves. No lasting physical harm resulted but it is a source of discussion within the group.

Stephan is 16 years old and involved in his church youth group. He became a Christian a year ago. Stephan is doing well at school and enjoys sporting activities like climbing, mountain biking and skateboarding. He and friends are planning a camping weekend in the hills. Some of his friends smoke cannabis occasionally and Stephan's parents cannot decide if he should go with them.

Motivation and Personality Type

We need to understand young people's motivations and aspirations, recognizing that personality differences affect attitudes to risk-taking behaviour. Some young people seem more inclined to endanger themselves than others.

Participation in risky activities may be the result of deficiency motivation or abundance motivation.[5] Deficiency motivation attracts individuals to behaviours that compensate for something they believe is lacking. This is often a significant motivation for young risk takers. Sarah might perceive that her parents do not love her because they are frequently absent. Her supposed lack of love motivates her to seek alternative forms of love (or sexual expressions of her understanding of love) in riskier settings. Aaron desires a peer group that provides belonging with apparent security so he participates in their risky activities. Not belonging may be riskier than belonging, despite possibilities of physical harm.

Abundance motivation refers to an individual's impulse to participate in activities that provide positive and stimulating peak experiences. For some young people, the potential thrill or satisfaction of participating in a particular activity induces them to believe they must do it to make life worth living. People labelled risk-averse are likelier to seek security and conformity through non-participation. For them the risks of negative consequences are too high to justify any potential benefit. Motivation is complicated, and often includes both deficiency and abundance. Studies demonstrate that adventurous young people who participate in certain activities, specifically those with abundance motivation, are more likely to develop higher levels of social and psychological competence, autonomy, independence, and decision making skills, but total risk avoidance is unhealthy for children's or young people's development. Some experimental risk taking should be tolerated.

Adventurous young people are more likely to develop higher levels of social competence

Peer Group Acceptance

A trinitarian God created us to belong within loving communities. This need is the motivating force behind most human behaviour. Young people's need to belong is important when considering their behaviour. Some risk taking behaviour is socially unacceptable yet may be a requirement of belonging to a particular community or peer group. A young person's willingness to self-harm with friends may allow them inclusion into that group. Willingness to ride a BMX recklessly in public places may secure inclusion and acceptance within another group.

As young people achieve individuation to become their own person they often rebel against familiar adult authority figures. Such behaviour inhibits that which they crave most—love, care and a place to belong with people they value—parents and carers. A belief that they are spurned by such adults motivates them to ensure they belong in other groups, by doing whatever it takes and to employ attention-seeking behaviour. Psychologist Abraham Maslow recognized that some rebellion is motivated by 'the profound hunger for group feelings, for contact, for real togetherness in the face of a common enemy, any enemy that can serve to form an amity group simply by posing an external threat.'[6] Parents may become this emnity group within youthful peer groups.

'Do not be afraid' is a common motif throughout the Bible. Some young people may appear fearless, and yet they are afraid of being excluded from significant communities. However, true discipleship and an authentic Christian spirituality cannot be dominated by the type of fear that holds many back from experiencing life and faith to the full—risk, sacrifice and self-giving commitment.

To Appear Adult

Adolescent development is a process of moving from childhood into adulthood. Young people want to be adult. In considering the list of risky behaviours we identified above we see that some dubious activities are socially acceptable within certain adult sub-cultures. Young people witness these sometimes acceptable adult behaviours and try emulate them to be adult themselves. Society can send confusing messages to the young. Underage alcohol abuse is common among adolescents. One survey in 2008 by the Institute for Public Policy Research (IPPR) discussed in *Time* magazine in April 2008 discovered 27% of 15-year-olds had been drunk 20 times or more.[7] Alcohol Concern research suggests that by age 13 a majority of teenagers drink alcohol, with the weekly alcohol consumption of 11–15-year-olds doubling to 10 units in 2004 since the early 90s. They

Society can send confusing messages to the young

further state that significant alcohol consumption by 18–24 year olds increases accidents, sexual risk taking and anti-social behaviour.

Use of recreational drugs, some of which seem to be widely acceptable within society despite their legal status, is also common. IPPR research suggests that 35% of 15-year-olds used cannabis within the previous year, while 40% of 15 year olds report experiencing sexual intercourse. The report highlights that British girls are the most sexually active in Europe, with over 15% foregoing contraception during sex. However, '...youth culture echoes and magnifies aspects of the adult world around it. Binge drinking, for example, is hardly the preserve of young Britons,'[8] as studies show with a third of British men and a fifth of British women drinking double the safe amount weekly.[9]

The glamourization of violence in films and computer games may lead young people to demonstrate violent (and therefore risky) behaviour in their real lives. Much research reflects how screen violence influences the young. Media representation of masculinity is often linked to the ability to drive, have sex with glamorous women or demonstrate power by violence. Within many western societies, lack of rites of passage may add to the need for young men to prove their manhood by participating in traditional male activities, with their associated risks.

Symbolic Identity

Finding a personal identity is a significant element of adolescent development. Our identities and how these are perceived by others are often created by the roles and titles we give ourselves or are given by others. If a young person is known as 'Wheelie King' because of an ability to pop wheelies on powerful motorbikes, his identity, and personal status, might well be based on this ability. Acceptance and praise from significant peers offeres motivation to continue and fortifies a sense of identity. Self-worth might also increase.

Anger and Release

We all get angry. To get angry is to be human. Young people are often labelled angry or destructive. However, young people have real issues, such as little opportunity for their voice to be heard in society, or unfair treatment. These things can lead to them expressing anger through risky behaviours.

Vavrik highlighted that anger towards society and local communities, combined with disaffection and alienation from school, was often vented in dangerous driving.[10] This explains my experience of young men involved in motor related crime in East London. Violence can release anger. Football hooliganism is an example of

Being angry does not mean being destructive

how risking personal harm by inflicting pain on others can sometimes release internal tensions and provide a buzz. Such fighting can become addictive.

Participation in physical activities and sports can help some young people express anger in disciplined and less destructive ways, but we must also provide contexts where young people can express feelings verbally, and support them in doing this constructively. Having trusting relationships with people who can ask pertinent questions and listen to responses is crucial for them. Being angry does not mean being destructive. Jesus got angry, but in ways that initiated personal and social transformations and the demolition of unjust systems and powers. We should learn from young people's passion for justice, and support them in expressing anger in creative and transformational ways.[11]

Suppressing Pain and Escaping 'Reality'

Physical or emotional pain is a fact of life. Many of us may take paracetamol for a headache, or have a drink after a hard day's work. Similarly, young people may choose different ways to seek to numb the pain or escape from tough lives.

Hope and Hopelessness

Hopelessness is an expectation that desired experiences are unlikely or that bad things will happen. Many young people believe that change is unlikely whatever they do—another feature of hopelessness. Regardless of their location, lack of control over life or future possibilities often results in reducing hope for young people. Hopelessness and depression occur in all communities, but young people experiencing economic deprivation are more susceptible to them. Hopelessness can bring such lack of self-worth that young people are discouraged from taking care of themselves—an obvious but frightening connection to risk taking behaviour. Young people who see little chance of gaining good jobs due to local unemployment are less likely to work hard at school. Limited educational motivation can foster behaviour that leads to exclusion. Exclusion gives more time on the streets with peers, resulting in temptations to practice anti-social behaviour. Any subsequent involvement with the criminal justice system reduces their chance of meaningful employment. Hopelessness can lead to risk taking behaviour that breeds further hopelessness. A significant role adults can play is helping young people to dream dreams and then supporting them to achieve them.

Adults can help young people to dream dreams and then support them to achieve them

The Adolescent Brain

Brain development is another factor associated with adolescent risk-taking behaviour. 'White matter,' nerve tissue which communicates between brain cells continues to develop from birth onwards. However, the grey matter—'the part of the brain responsible for processing information—the "thinking" part—develops quickly during childhood and slows in adolescence, with the frontal and temporal lobes the last to mature.'[12] However, the prefrontal cortex is where executive functions, such as planning, judgment, reasoning and impulse control occur. While young people may be able to understand risks in a one-to-one discussion, in the heat of the moment, reasoning components may be less effective. Teenage brains also have higher levels of dopamine, a neurotransmitter which relates to 'pleasure, movement and sexual desire' and might, according to Underwood, '...increase the need for extra stimulation through risk taking.' Focusing on physiological or psychological or sociological aspects in isolation would be naïve. We need to recognize that all three factors often play a part.

Young People's Perspectives

Hearing young people's perspective is important. Frontier Youth Trust spent time discussing with young people their involvement in a range of activities, and their perceptions of both the risks and benefits involved. The activities the young people listed included biking, climbing, skim-boarding, surfing, creek-jumping, skiing, boxing, power-boating, sky-diving, football, sailing and hockey. These are all deemed acceptable activities and may provide positive experiences and the potential for learning and growth but all contain an element of risk.

The most common reason young people stated for taking up these activities was the excitement they experienced, with peer influence to participate also being a major factor. Reduction of boredom was significant for many young people questioned. Peer influence and the reduction of boredom may be forms of deficit motivation, although they may not be overly problematic in cases such as these. Significant benefits from the young people's perspectives included: the buzz out of something that demands skill; increased respect from others; gaining new friends; the acquisition of new skills; increased self-image and self-confidence. It is clear that motivation to participate in activities can be mixed.

Motivation to participate in activities can be mixed

When the age of participants was examined it became clear that generally older young people (17–20 year olds in this case) were better able to recognize and transfer learning from their participation in certain activities into other areas of their lives. Transferable skills expressed by the young people included: increased self-control; better control of fear; more confidence; increased motivation and determination (due to long distance cycling); better problem solving skills and leadership experience.

Often what is needed is a context in which the activity and its potential learning can be discussed within individual or small group settings. This requires skilled facilitators who are able to support young people to articulate, explore and reflect on their experiences. Once learning has been identified it may be transferred through the use of role-play and discussion, so young people recognize how they may use their learning within more complex, everyday settings. For example, communication skills used within a problem solving activity such as raft-building may be transferred into an everyday conflict situation, helping young people develop conflict-resolution strategies.

The Gap Project—Self-Harm Support Group

A recent national inquiry into self-harm among young people stated that an effective strategy to recovery from self-harm is understanding from others, and peer support. Recognizing a lack of such provision in their community, *The Gap Project,* run by Bethnal Green Mission Church with the support of local mental health services, developed a peer support group for young women aged 13–19 involved in self-harming behaviour. The group focuses on providing a safe space to explore issues surrounding their self-injury and facilitating the young people to support each other in this process. Hannah Harniess, the Self-Injury Support Group Coordinator, highlights the fact that 'self-harm is such a huge issue (affecting at least 1 in 15 young people), and is so often mishandled and misunderstood.' She is encouraged that 'churches and Christian organizations are taking a more proactive approach,' recognizing the need for partnership between churches and existing mental health services as crucial. There are many legal, ethical and good practice considerations that need to be taken into account in this type of work, but there are also structures and services in place to support this type of ministry. The need is significant, and the services all too often limited.

4 Harm Reduction Interventions

Understanding why young people participate in risky activities helps us support them, to reduce potential harm. We should be realistic about real risks as well as perceived risks, remembering that when discussing risky behaviour with adolescents, perception is key.

Play England states, 'Children need and want to take risks when they play,' with play provision '…offering children stimulating, challenging environments for exploring and developing their abilities.'[13] This principle also applies to adolescents. Adam Voce of Play England highlights the importance of adventurous play in developing critical life skills, stating that 'constantly wrapping children (and young people) in cotton wool can leave them ill equipped to deal with stressful or challenging situations they might encounter later in life.'[14]

What Are the Risks?

Different activities within different contexts bring different risks. Competencies and experience are also significant. In some contexts—like supervised outdoor pursuit activities (climbing, hiking, kayaking etc) or activities/games within youth clubs—risk levels may be managed so young people safely experience adventure and excitement. Risk remains but with minimal danger. The contexts where adolescents experiment (with drug and alcohol use for example), increase or reduce potential harm, with some activities and contexts precluding satisfactory risk management opportunities. People concerned with preventing lasting harm to young people should think creatively about risk and harm reduction in unmanaged contexts.

Risk Assessment

These questions may help when considering young people's participation in risky activities, whatever the context, and with whatever possible levels of management.

- What is the possibility of injury or death?
- What factors contribute to increased likelihood of harm? For example, presence of alcohol, location, time, with whom the activity takes place.
- What could happen to young participants?

- What possibility exists for minor injury? Are permanent consequences possible?
- Do emotional/psychological/spiritual risks accompany particular activities or experiences?
- Is the young person aware of these risks?
- What potential benefits can occur from participation? What lessons are possible?
- Individually, as an organization, or as a community, how can we reduce risks to young people?
- Is immediate intervention required or are longer term strategies more appropriate?
- Who else should be involved in interventions?

Such questions could form part of risk assessments by organizations. Awareness reduces the potential of serious harm to adolescents in our care.[15]

Adult moral compasses may differ from those of young people, and faith perspectives may affect attitudes towards certain behaviours. This can lead young people to consider us moralistic and judgmental if we communicate carelessly.

Other Issues to Consider for Practice

- Who is responsible for the safety and wellbeing of those involved in activities you facilitate? Who has current first aid training? Are leaders aware of appropriate actions in various circumstances?
- Are there enough leaders to ensure that risks of physical, emotional or sexual harm to young people are reduced?
- Are risk assessments completed and documented for all your events? If someone is injured, do you have procedures to deal with the situation?
- If you saw a young person about to participate in an activity that was dangerous for them or others, how would you choose your response?

Grafted is a project is based in Newcastleton, a village of about 900 people in the Scottish Borders. It uses outdoor activities such as canoeing, mountain biking and mountaineering with young offenders and chaotic young people in an attempt to 'give hope to those without hope.' *Grafted* is supported by a partnership of the Church Army, In2Venture and Barnabas Trust and has been instrumental in developing a 'fresh church' in Newcastleton, and through its current programme, *Window of Time,* aims at developing leadership and self-esteem in chaotic young people. (www.grafted.co.uk)

5 Getting Involved with Young Risk Takers

We cannot always convince young people of the 'error of their ways' and persuade them to stop the activities they find enjoyable and beneficial. Yet there are ways that individuals and members of faith communities can reduce harmful outcomes. Jesus has harsh words for those who cause children and young people to sin, and for those who do not welcome them (Matt 18.5–6; Mark 9.42; Luke 17.1–2). Here are some suggested ways to influence the lives of young people and the community:

- Avoid denial. We can be unaware of risks young people take because of a reluctance to admit that our young people are involved in risky activities. We need to be honest.
- Develop non-judgmental and non-blame attitudes. Having the ability to look beyond drug use or other risk behaviour to see the individual and their needs is the first and most important step in developing potentially transformative relationships.
- Be prepared to visit young people's contexts. This can give us a voice that may be heard, thus challenging media suggestions that Britain is scared of its young and helping to prophetically reverse that trend.[16] Exploring ways of becoming involved in detached youth work within the community can familiarize one with local adolescents.[17] Other methods include smiling at young people rather than frowning or crossing the road. Try catching a young person off guard by asking them how they are, and be prepared to listen to their answer—maybe you will both be pleasantly surprised.
- Develop awareness of issues facing young people. Your understanding of drugs, alcohol and sexually transmitted diseases might encourage them to seek your opinion. Within trusting and confidential relationships young people may be more co-operative and responsive. Awareness of specific patterns and contexts of risk behaviours that individuals practise is helpful.
- Know what specialized support services are available, either directly or through referral, for adolescents. These could include youth counselling services, youth work projects offering guidance

on specific issues including legal advice. Most GP surgeries, Citizens Advice Bureaux and libraries will have relevant information.

- Provide young people with opportunities to articulate their experiences and how these influence attitudes to risky behaviour. This may happen one-to-one, but could expand into small peer support groups.
- Understand issues of confidentiality and the child/youth/vulnerable adult policies of your church or organization. Young people need to express their needs within safe contexts. Having a group/community approach to intervention and support is helpful. Much adolescent risk behaviour takes place within community contexts.
- Recognize that young people normally obtain their closest support and care within their family. Youth workers easily lose sight of this, despite their person-centred approaches to youth work and ministry. Involve families in support processes with the young person's consent.
- Within youth projects or mentoring relationships, encourage the acquisition of skills and attitudes that support personal development. These include communication skills—including the ability and willingness to discuss emotions and feelings, decision making skills and negotiation and problem solving skills. Encourage attitudes and beliefs such as self-worth and aspiration. Offer support to achieve realistic dreams.
- Develop a commitment to explore how church communities, and not just youth leaders, can be involved in supporting personal, social, educational and spiritual development of young people in the local community.
- Residentials (camps or trips) are risky for young people as they are away from their safe environment, where they have coping and survival strategies. Putting young people into stressful situations, where they cannot easily run away, often causes them to react, and release bottled up tension, anger and frustration. Whilst residentials can be difficult with young people involved in risk-taking behaviour, they can provide opportunities for deeper relationships with youth workers and occasions to explore deeper issues that may lead to harm reduction alternatives.

Practical Steps Churches Can Take

- Develop youth programmes that appeal to young people within the church and to those on the fringes of society.
- Use adventure-based activities that create abundance/peak experiences as one element of youth provision, ensuring that links between the activity and personal and social learning are clear. This requires experience and planning but is necessary to maximize learning potential.
- Include lists of youth support services (health, counselling, guidance, activity or issue-based projects) for young people on prominent notice boards in church.
- Participate in campaigns and activities to increase youth provision in the community, for example adventure playgrounds, sports facilities, youth clubs etc and promote young people's positive contribution to society.
- Encourage church members to volunteer to assist existing youth projects that young people from your community access.

Street Pastors

A significant way churches can engage with young risk-takers is through projects such as street pastors. The idea is that groups of local Christians become temporary pastors to those in need within town and city centres, particularly in the early hours of the morning, when many young people are prone to the excesses of drugs and alcohol. Teams of pastors might find themselves helping people in physical, emotional and spiritual need, meeting them at their point of need and offering unconditional care and practical support. A significant additional benefit of participation in such projects is that the church becomes aware of the needs of members of its local community and is able to provide appropriate practical support. The church might earn local credibility with other services and people. Street pastors are people who cross over the road in order to help those in need.

Detached Youth Work

Detached youth work is one of many youth work models that can support young people involved in risky behaviour. Unlike many models of youth work and ministry, detached youth work meets young people in the places where they congregate—parks, local estates, shopping centres, streets or graveyards.

Unlike outreach work, which seeks to invite young people to specific events, clubs or other activities, detached youth work aims to support young people unconditionally, 'where they are at.' Richard Passmore describes detached youth work as a 'versatile, non-threatening, young-person-centred approach to youth work' which can be 'highly effective in both urban and rural settings, and is an important tool for reaching young people that the church would not normally come into contact with.'[18] In essence, detached workers become guests on young people's turf, relinquishing the power a building (with its associated rules) holds, and the positional power of the leader.

6 A Theology and Spirituality of Risk Taking

Shane Claiborne says suburbs frighten him more than the city, due to Jesus' comment in Matthew 10.28 not to fear things like violence and crime that can harm the body but fear things that harm the soul. Hebrews 11 shows clearly that the life of faith is a life of risk, with a catalogue of risky ventures that would never have been undertaken by people concerned first for personal safety.[19] Modern Christianity has become risk-averse, and houses subtler demonic forces—numbness, complacency, comfort—that can eat away at our souls.[20] Tom Wright tells of a bishop who complained that he had less impact than the apostles who caused riots wherever they went, saying that wherever he went they served tea.[21]

The Old Testament prophets took risks, spoke and enacted unpopular messages to kings of their times.[22] Today, 'Young people are among God's most forthright, frustrating, and often unwitting prophets, reminding us that salvation is at stake, for they will not give up on true love until they find it, or until consumer culture numbs them into a lobotomized compliance, whichever comes first.'[23] We must learn about true discipleship and the cost of true love from adventurous and passionate young people. A college professor once warned his students that too many of us, '…tiptoe through life in order to arrive at death safely.'[24] We need more youthful reckless abandon. In my experience reckless abandonment has not featured in church teaching. It means taking risks. Jesus did not tiptoe through life. Perhaps it is young people, within and beyond the church, who can teach us the attitude of Jesus. If we called ourselves followers of Jesus rather than Christians, with the social, political and historical baggage this term holds, maybe we would recognize the hazards involved in true discipleship.

Future Hope

One characteristic of adolescent risk-takers is living for the moment due to lack of future hope and fatalistic attitudes. Interestingly, the Western church has fallen into the same trap. Without an eternal perspective we seem unwilling to habitually follow Jesus, being unprepared to risk and sacrifice as radical disciples. When we see ourselves as temporary strangers in a strange land we will see that our destination provides a means to participate in the way of Christ.

Hope, as Walter Brueggemann suggests, is '…the refusal to accept the reading of reality which is the majority opinion; and one does that only at great political and existential risk.'[25] When physical, emotional, economic, social or religious security and comfort cease to dominate our decision making, we will model a more radical, attractive and accepting faith, one that might attract young people. Brueggemann further states that, 'Hope is subversive, for it limits the grandiose pretention of the present, daring to announce that the present to which we have all made commitments is now called into question.' Young risk-takers might be subversive. They might live for the moment. They also show us what it means to risk losing to make important gains. Maybe what young people crave is more akin to the pearl of great worth than we give them credit for. Was building a community of risk takers what Jesus meant for his church? Much in the New Testament suggests this.

Urban Expression (www.urbanexpression.org.uk) has developed a number of values that relate not only to urban church planting but to mission in general. One such value is that of taking risks, recognizing that it is acceptable to fail. Other values include the recognition of Christian faith as a journey, being committed to helping people who are frequently marginalized, condemned and abused by society move forward from wherever they are at present. *Urban Expression* also challenges the trend of some Christians moving out of the cities and encourage Christians to relocate to the inner cities, despite the so-called risks. Being prepared to take risks with people, by being involved in their often messy lives, bears likeness to the incarnation. Recognizing that we will often not succeed in preventing young people from damaging risk taking must not become a reason to disengage. Jesus still looked into the eyes of the rich man and loved him (Mark 10.21). In fact, acknowledging personal weakness, insecurities and failings will enable us relate to young people experiencing similar emotions. If we communicate that it is wrong to acknowledge when we mess up, how will young people learn integrity, relate to us and learn from their experiences?

Doing Theology as Risk-Taking Behaviour

Kenneth Leech suggests that, 'Only a theology which is marked by the spirit of adventure, the urge to discovery and the practice of pilgrimage, rather than one which is static and propositional, (not taking any risks…or indeed having any faith) can respond to people in transition and upheaval.'[26] Adolescents therefore require risk taking within their theologizing, their search for meaning, and their understanding of God. They ask questions adults avoid. Most of us would agree that being adult does not necessarily lead to wise leadership and stewardship. Empowering children and young people to become involved in church decision-making processes may be risky but as those who are less risk-averse they may be more faithful to the true call of the church, to work towards the prophetic transformation of society according to God's vision and purpose.

The incarnation demonstrates God's willingness to risk and experience pain and suffering for humanity's sake. Despite opposition Jesus broke down social, cultural, religious and political boundaries. Because Jesus risked social and religious exclusion he was executed as a radical, rebelling against contemporary power structures. Young risk-takers, when appropriately supported and discipled, might relate to Jesus in ways that we cannot or will not, and teach us valuable lessons. Jesus' risk-taking demonstrated the ultimate sacrifice which may attract young people who have not found true love. Rather than seeking retaliation against those who had rejected him, God sought restoration. He desired relationship, or as Miroslav Volf would suggest, embrace, rather than exclusion. Rather than seeking young people's continued exclusion by retaliating against their behaviour—often initially caused by a failure of society to recognize their very real needs—in punitive ways, maybe a more creative, positive and transformative approach would be to seek reconciliation and restoration with marginalized young risk-takers.

Church on the Edge is a partnership between CMS, the Diocese of Exeter and local churches in association with Bristol Centre for Youth Ministry and Frontier Youth Trust. It aims to develop 'a fresh approach to challenging young people's behaviour through good youth work processes with the critical intention to grow a relevant expression of church with marginalized young people. It works through building meaningful and purposeful relationships; developing community through contact, support, trips and residential experiences; engaging in rites of passage and developing culturally relevant expressions of church.

Implications for Ministry with Young People

What are we trying to achieve in our ministry with young people? Do we want them to be safe or do we want them to affect their world by supporting them to hear the call of God, to become involved in the messiness of people's lives? Rather than putting on more safe programmes we need young people to plan and implement projects that transform people's lives, including their own. Perhaps we should be more concerned with protecting them from apathy and comfort. I once saw a T-shirt which stated that, 'Jesus came not only to comfort the disturbed, but to disturb the comfortable.' If we recognize risks associated with simply entertaining young people and teaching them stories, namely the potential of causing them to sin by their inaction, we will be convicted by the words of Jesus in Matthew 18.5.

Young people's passion needs to be harnessed if it is to be used in transformative, rather than destructive, ways. When our commitment is caught up with the passion God has for them, and his creative imagination is coupled with the resources of his church, when his people are no longer reluctant to cross over the street due to fear, then maybe the church will be relevant in the way it is called to be.

Oasis Trust, BMS World Mission, Youth for Christ, and many more Christian organizations, as well as churches, offer young people the opportunity to put their faith into action. Short and mid-term mission programmes in the UK and around the world, provide the context in which followers of Jesus can risk discomfort and challenge, as they seek to demonstrate God's love to the often unloved. www.oasisuk.org; www.bmsworldmission.org; www.yfc.co.uk

Questions for Reflection

- What risky behaviours do you see in young people you encounter?
- What are young people's perceived benefits from participation in risky behaviour? Can their behaviour be rationalized?
- In what ways might we sometimes over-protect the young?
- In what areas of your life are there risks? How do you decide if the risk is worth taking?
- In what ways is following Jesus risky for you? How do you help young people understand a spirituality of risk-taking as part of their journey of faith in Jesus?
- What risks should we encourage young people to take through our actions and teaching?
- What is the balance between encouraging and empowering young people towards risky mission settings and being responsible for their safety?
- How can we relate to perceived overly protective parents of Jesus followers, who themselves are Christians?
- In what ways does fear of young people limit the kingdom building initiatives of God's mission to all the people of the world?
- If the church (*ie* its members) is not out there in their local communities, what relevance has the gospel to young risk takers?

Notes

1 E Gullone and S Moore, 'Adolescent Risk Taking and the Five-factor Model of Personality' in *Journal of Adolescence* 2000, 23, pp 393-407.

2 The Play England research explores benefits and challenges in enabling children to manage personal risks whilst playing. See the Play England website: http://www.playday.org.uk/playday_campaigns/2008_give_us_a_go/2008_research.aspx

3 'Over-cautious parents stop play' http://news.bbc.co.uk/1/hi/uk/7540076.stm Accessed 4th August 2008.

4 Certain self-harming behaviour (particularly among girls) has been identified as taking place within peer groups. If a young person is discovered practising self-harming behaviour others within their peer group may do likewise.

5 J Rowan, *Ordinary Ecstasy—Humanistic Psychology in Action* (London: Routledge, 1988) p 247.

6 A Maslow, *Motivation and Personality* (third edition) (New York: Harper Collins, 1987) p 20.

7 By the Institute for Public Policy Research (IPPR) discussed in *Time* magazine in April 2008.

8 See Alcohol Concern, www.alcoholconcern.org.uk

9 C Mayer, 'Mean Streets,' *Time* magazine, 7 April 2008, pp 34-40.

10 J Vavrik 'Personality and risk-taking: a brief report on adolescent male drivers' in *Journal of Adolescence* 1997, 20, pp 461-465.

11 K C Dean, *Practising Passion: Youth and the Quest for a Passionate Church* (Cambridge: Eerdmans, 2004).

12 N Underwood, 'The Teenage Brain: Why Adolescents Sleep In, Take Risks, and Won't Listen to Reason' http://www.walrusmagazine.com/articles/2006.11-science-the-teenage-brain. Accessed 2nd September 2008.

13 Play England, *Managing Risk in Play Provision: A Position Statement*, http://www.playengland.org.uk

14 http://www.playengland.org.uk

15 An example of questions relating to drug use can be found in the online resources for this booklet.

16 Matt 18.5-6; Mark 9.42; Luke 17.1-2.

17 Front cover of *Time*, 7 April 2008.

18 See R Passmore, *Meet Them Where They're At* (Milton Keynes: Scripture Union, 2003) p 21.

19 Passmore, p 21.

20 *Dictionary of Biblical Imagery* (Leicester: IVP, 1998) p 729.

21 S Claiborne, *The Irresistible Revolution* (Grand Rapids: Zondervan, 2006) p 227.

22 T Wright, *Acts for Everyone Part 1* (London: SPCK, 2008) p 61.

23 *Dictionary of Biblical Imagery* (Leicester: IVP, 1998) p 729.

24 Dean, p 6.

25 *ibid*, p 225.

26 W Brueggemann, *The Prophetic Imagination* (Minneapolis: Fortress Press, 2001) p 65.

27 Mark 10.21.

28 K Leech, *Doing Theology in Altab Ali Park* (London: DLT, 2006).